T0132101

Little James' Big Adventures

The Globe
Janine Iannelli

Illustrated by: Michelle Iannelli

To order additional copies of this book, contact:
Xlibris
1-888-795-4274
www.Xlibris.com
Orders@Xlibris.com

ISBN: 978-1-6641-2635-0 (sc)
ISBN: 978-1-6641-2636-7 (hc)
ISBN: 978-1-6641-2634-3 (e)

Print information available on the last page

Rev. date: 08/18/2020

Little James dreams of places far far away,

That he hopes to visit and see one day.

Like Europe, Africa, Australia and more!

Like Asia, South America and Antarctica for sure!

Christmas is approaching and Santa will soon be on his way.

I need to talk to Santa, thinks James, *today today today!*

They go to visit Santa,

James doesn't waste any time.

He runs right up to Santa,

And onto his lap he climbs.

"What can I get you little James? I see you've been a good boy.
What would you like for Christmas this year, tell me what kind of toy?"

"I don't want a toy at all," James said.
"I want an adventure, I want that instead.

I want to see the world, visit old cities and new.
I want to see everything and take my sister too."

"Well," says Santa, "I'm going to have to think,

Keep being a good boy," he says and gives James a wink.

On Christmas Eve night James is too excited to sleep.

He tries to relax, he tries to count sheep.

James mind can't stop wondering, *what will it be what will it be?!*
Maybe a ticket around the world, oh all the things he will see!

Or will Santa himself be outside with his sleigh?
And then take him to different places each day?

Or will he get his own reindeer, or his own private plane?
Or maybe a magic carpet, or broom stick or a flying candy cane?

Finally it's morning and James runs towards the tree,

He looks underneath to see what it could be.

And there with a twinkle is a small box wrapped with a bow,

He tears through the paper, at last he will know!

He opens the lid and takes a look inside,

It's a snow globe of the world that reads, 'Enjoy the ride!'

James doesn't understand, surely this globe can't fly,

It can't take him anywhere, James tries not to cry.

The north pole floats in the arctic on sea ice and is not considered a country or continent.

Later that night James and his sister Susie get tucked in,
Little James looks at the globe and then his frown turns to a grin.

"Well Susie," James laughs, "at least it's not coal.
Though I do wish I could talk to Santa, but he's all the way in The North Pole."

Then all of a sudden the ground beneath them starts to shake,
James and Susie grab each other tight, "Oh no is this an earth quake?"

The walls begin to tremble, and the floor starts to rumble!
Then they're sucked into the floor where they both begin to tumble!

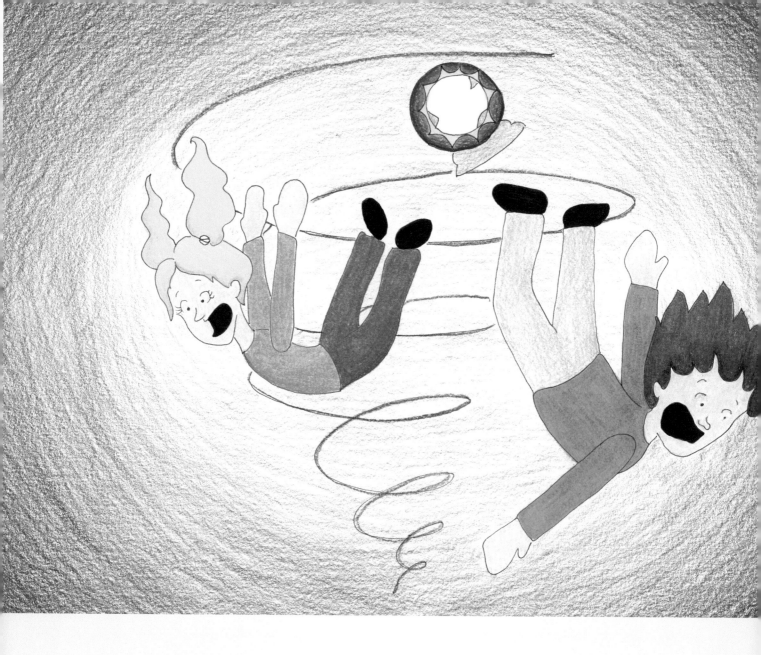

"Ahhhhhhhh!"

Then suddenly it's still, and they open up their eyes,
"Ho Ho Ho!" Laughs Santa, "Well, what a lovely surprise!"

James can't believe it, his Christmas wish came true!
And now he's here in Santa's workshop and he's with his sister too.

Jingle bells are jingling, and the smell of hot cocoa is in the air,

The whole workshop is twinkling, and the elves are everywhere.

The list reads:

James
Susie
Rodrigo
Aniste
Brooke
Mikey
Marisa
Cheyenne
Sven
Mehdi
Gia
Tomaso

"Now being you're here says Santa, how about a little tour?
I'll show you around the workshop, the reindeer, the elves and much more!"

The elves show them around and how they make toys,
And Santa points out the list of all the good girls and boys.

The North Pole has two seasons winter and summer. During the summer, there is sunlight all day; during the winter, it is always dark.

Next they walk outside and notice they're floating on ice!
"That's the North Pole for you," says Santa, "and in winter its dark all day and night."

"Wow!" says James, as he looks all around.
"There really is no solid ground!"

"Hey James look! Check it out over there!"

"Oh wow Susie!" James gasps, "That's a polar bear!"

The arctic fox has the warmest pelt of any animal in the arctic.

Six seal species live in the Arctic: harp, hooded, ringed, bearded, spotted, and ribbon.

Walrus are huge and can weigh up to 1.5 tons! Also, both male and female Walrus have tusks and can live up to 40 years in the wild.

There are 17 different species of whales in the arctic but Belugas, Bowheads, and Narwhals are the only whales to inhabit Arctic waters all year round.

"If you think that's cool," says Santa, "then meet our whole crew!

Check out the Walrus and seals, the fox and whales too!"

"Woah this is amazing!" Says James.

"It is!" Susie shouts.

"But I don't see any penguins out and about."

"Ho Ho," laughs Santa, "you won't find any penguins up here. They only hang out in the Southern Hemisphere."

The average temperature in the winter in the North Pole is -40 degrees Fahrenheit (-40C) and is actually warmer than the South Pole!

"I'm cold," says Susie, "can we go back inside?"

Santa wraps her in a blanket and says, "First let's take a ride!"

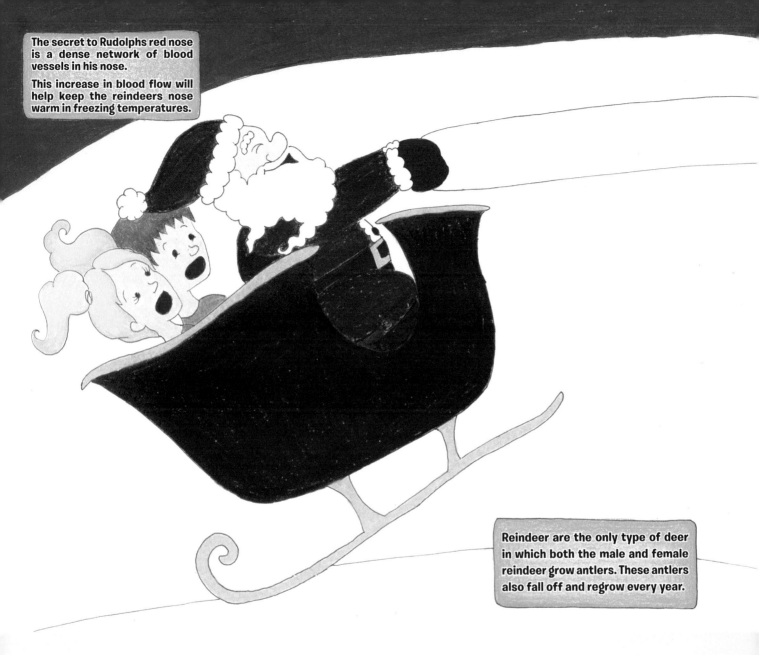

The secret to Rudolphs red nose is a dense network of blood vessels in his nose.

This increase in blood flow will help keep the reindeers nose warm in freezing temperatures.

Reindeer are the only type of deer in which both the male and female reindeer grow antlers. These antlers also fall off and regrow every year.

The reindeer come running and they're scooped up into the sleigh,

Santa laughs as they take off and yells, "Up up and away!"

They soar over the workshop till they're up very high,
The jingle bells jangle as they fly through the sky.

The stars are a-twinkling and the moon shines so bright,
Then they look down and oh what a sight!

It's a wonder land of houses all sparkly and a glow,

They stare down in silence and admire the world below.

They fly over Russia, Finland and Sweden.
They fly over Norway, Iceland, and Greenland.

They soar over Canada and James fills up with glee,
"I can't believe all the places I'll see!"

"Oh Santa," they say, "thank you for this amazing night!"
"You're welcome kids but let's get you home before it's light!"

The sleigh lands on their roof and Santa hugs them goodbye.
"But wait," says James, "how do we get back inside?"

"That's what the globe is for," says Santa, "so now wherever you roam,
Just place your hands on the globe and say home sweet home!"

Find out where little James' magic snow globe takes him next!
www.Janinelannelli.com

Follow me on Instagram! @Janinelannelliauthor

Printed in the United States
By Bookmasters